I Wish I Were a Fairy Tale

A Story Illustrated with Cakes

WRITTEN AND ILLUSTRATED BY
CRYSTAL WALTERS

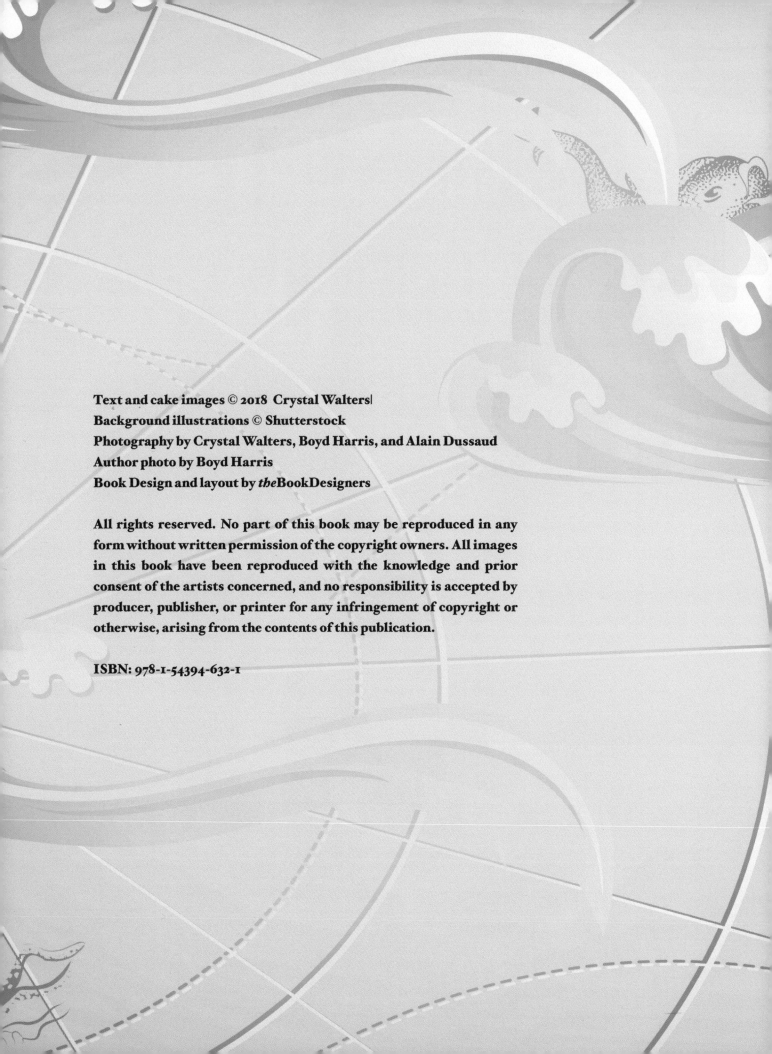

ISBN: 978-1-54394-632-1

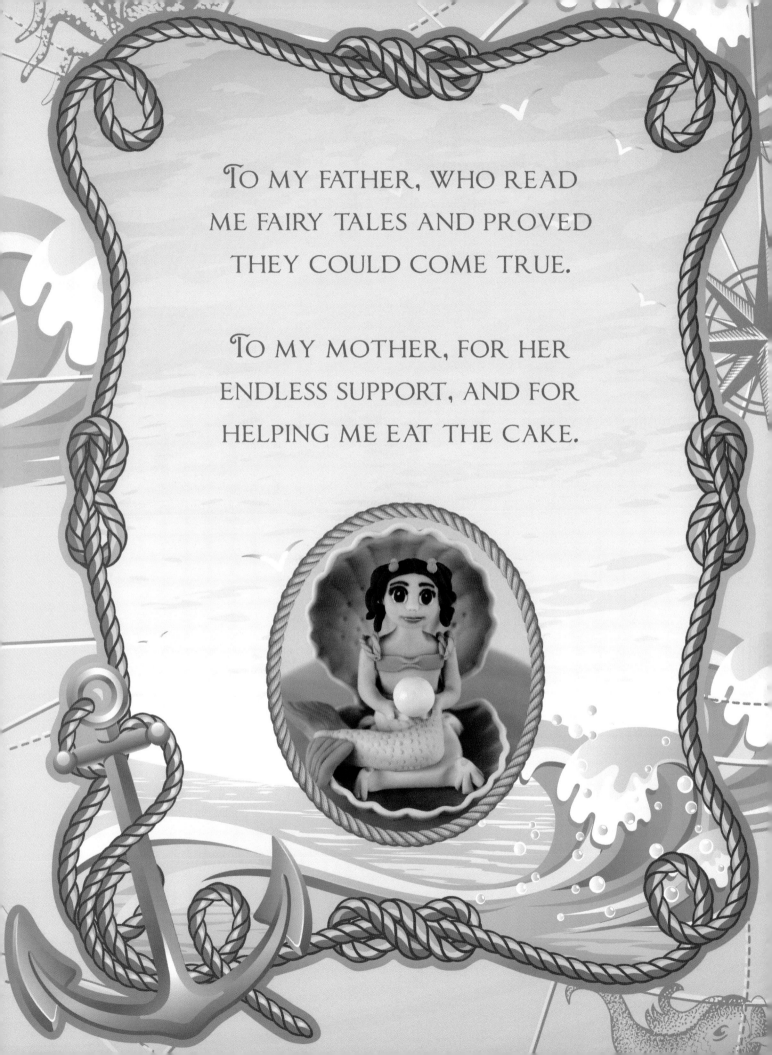

To my father, who read me fairy tales and proved they could come true.

To my mother, for her endless support, and for helping me eat the cake.

I WISH I WERE A FAIRY TALE WITH MAGIC EVERY DAY.

I'D FLY AROUND ON FAIRY WINGS AND ALL I'D DO IS PLAY.

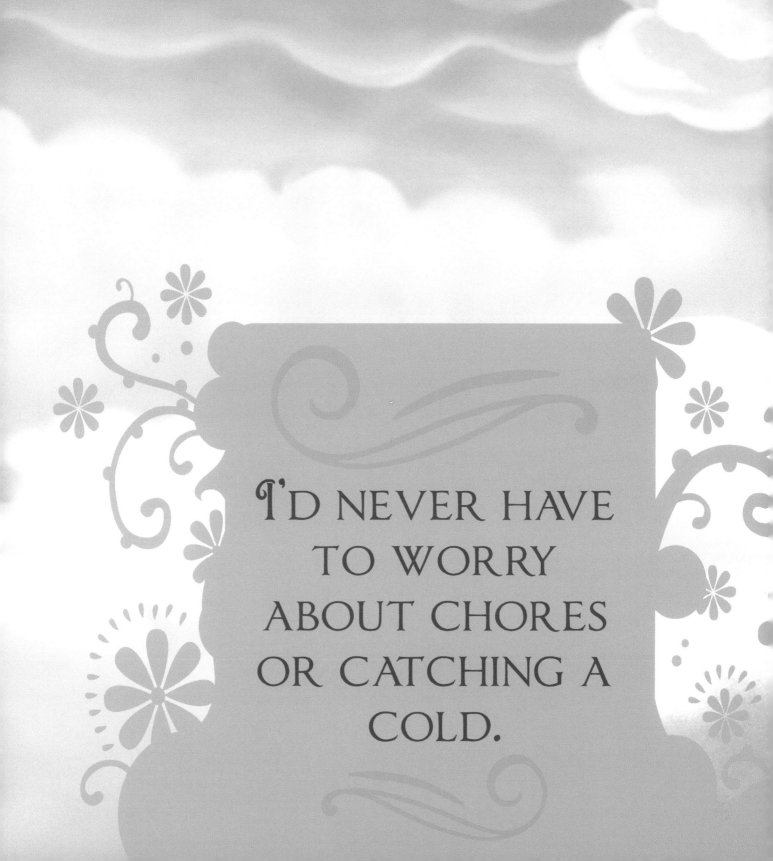

I'D NEVER HAVE TO WORRY ABOUT CHORES OR CATCHING A COLD.

I'D SWIM THE SEA
WITH MERMAIDS
AND HOLD A
REAL PEARL IN
MY HAND.

I WOULD EVEN BECOME A PRINCESS AND RULE A FARAWAY LAND.

I'D VISIT SNOW WHITE AND HER SEVEN DWARFS WHO'D INSIST I STAY FOR TEA.

I'D FLOAT ON CLOUDS WITH UNICORNS, OH WHAT FUN THAT WOULD BE!

EACH NIGHT AS
THE MOON COMES
UP AND THE STARS
TWINKLE AND GLOW,
I'D GO ON A TRIP
WITH THE SANDMAN
TO VISIT OTHER
CHILDREN
AND SAY,
'HELLO!'

I'D HELP THEM LIVE THEIR OWN ADVENTURES AS THEY READ MY FAIRY TALE, AND HELP THEM ALL FALL ASLEEP AS THEIR DREAMS SET SAIL.

THEY WOULD DREAM
THE DREAMS OF
HAPPINESS AND OF
TIMES LONG AGO,
STORIES THEY COULD
REVISIT WHEN THEY
ARE FEELING LOW.

I'D HELP MAKE THEIR
WORLD AN ENCHANTED
PLACE ONE TALE AT A
TIME. I'D BRING MAGIC
INTO THEIR WORLD
WITH JUST THIS SIMPLE
RHYME.

FOR THE BEST THING
ABOUT FAIRY TALES IS I'D
GET TO BE A PART
OF THE SPECIAL STORIES
THAT LIVE INSIDE EACH
CHILD'S HEART.
FOR EVEN WHEN IT'S
TIME FOR ME TO SAY
GOODBYE TO YOU,
PICKING UP MY BOOK AGAIN
IS ALL YOU'D HAVE TO DO!
I'D BE RIGHT HERE WAITING
FOR YOU TO TAKE MY HAND,
SO WE CAN FLY AWAY
TOGETHER INTO
A FANTASY LAND.

FOR THE TRUTH IS
THAT FAIRY TALES
NEVER REALLY END,
FOR WHEN THEY ARE
READ AND LOVED,
THEY BECOME YOUR
SWEETEST FRIEND!

A NOTE ABOUT THE ILLUSTRATION

When it came time to illustrate this book, I decided to do something very different: Instead of paper and ink, I wanted to use frosting and fondant! Just like a classic children's book, each page shows the main character acting out the words of the story, but it just so happens that all the characters in this tale are made out of sugar, and their settings are carved out of cake. Some cakes in this book are created in a classic tiered fashion, while others are shaped to resemble magical settings such as a fairy's tree house or a smiling moon. Still, no matter how they are sculpted on the outside, on the inside they are all cake. Each one has its own flavor and frosting, such as a vanilla cake with chocolate buttercream, or a double-chocolate cake filled with a cookie crumble frosting. All the cakes are covered with fondant, an edible sugar paste. The characters are also made out of fondant, which makes everything on each cake edible, from the dragon to the flowers, to the smallest flags on the castle's towers! I hope you enjoy this delicious style of illustration.

ACKNOWLEDGMENTS

I created nearly eighty handmade sugar sculptures for *I Wish I Were A Fairy Tale*, and not one of them would have been completed if it were not for the love and encouragement of my mother, Lucette Walters. Thank you for your artistic eye, and for being the perfect combination of mom and friend.

To my brilliant niece, Raya, who was the inspiration for the main character, and who is just as sweet.

To Natasha Young, whose friendship is as magical as a rainbow-unicorn cake floating on cotton candy topped with strawberry sprinkles.

To Alain, for helping me with the photographs.

To the creative team at *the*BookDesigners whose talent took my vision to the next level.

To Boyd Harris, who makes me want to create more cakes just so he can photograph them.

Finally, to my eternal puppy, Ma Petite, who followed me through every fairy tale.